The Screaming Chef

A picture book

Written by Peter Ackerman

Illustrated by Max Dalton

David R. Godine, *Publisher · Boston*

First published in 2017 by
David R. Godine, Publisher
Post Office Box 450
Jaffrey, New Hampshire 03452
www.godine.com

Library of Congress Cataloging-in-Publication Data

Names: Ackerman, Peter, author. | Dalton, Max, illustrator.
Title: The Screaming Chef : a picture book / written Peter Ackerman ;
illustrated by Max Dalton.
Description: Jaffrey, New Hampshire : David R. Godine - Publisher, 2017. |
Summary: A young boy who screams except while eating takes over the
cooking, and proves so talented that his parents open a restaurant
with him as head chef.
Identifiers: LCCN 2016050113 | ISBN 9781567925982 (alk. paper)
Subjects: | CYAC: Behavior--Fiction. | Cooks--Fiction. | Restaurants-
-Fiction.
Classification: LCC PZ7.A18255 Scr 2017 | DDC [E]--dc23
LC record available at https://lccn.loc.gov/2016050113

First printing, 2017
Printed at Toppan Leefung Printing Ltd. in China

Once upon a time
there was a boy
who wouldn't stop...

He screamed when he went to bed.

He screamed when he went to school.

He screamed when his ice-cream cone fell on the floor.

He screamed when he lost his teddy bear.

The boy screamed so much he was driving his parents bananas.

They tried everything to make him stop.

They gave him Time Outs. He screamed.

They gave him Time Ins.
He screamed.

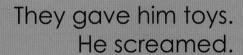

They gave him toys.
He screamed.

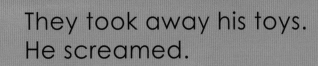

They took away his toys.
He screamed.

The only time the boy didn't scream...

6

...was when he was eating.

His father's
chickpea curry
melted his mouth.

His mother's
succulent soup
made his belly feel
like a soft, warm pillow.

And their linguini...
Well, his parents'
linguini was
so luscialicious that
the boy tipped over
on the floor and fell
asleep for a week.

All the eating made the boy so happy that his parents kept feeding him. But by spring, he couldn't fit through the door.

One night, when his parents were running late from work, they rushed making dinner and burned the chicken. The boy started to scream.

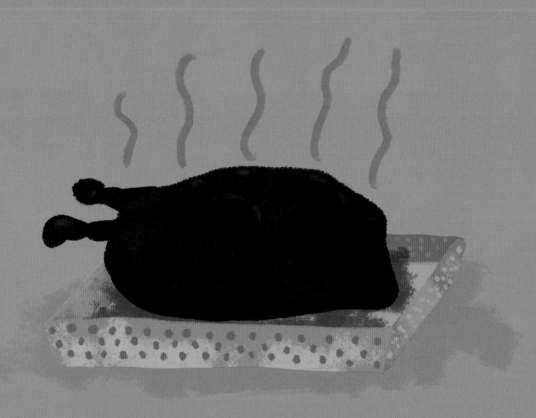

This time his mother couldn't take it. "That's it." she said.
"If you don't like the food then cook it yourself."

So the boy started to cook.

He cut carrots and diced daikons.

He filleted fish and baked beans.

He flavored stews and sautéed succotash.

The boy was so busy cooking he forgot to eat.

He was having so
much fun he started
to sing. And his cooking
became so good...

...his parents opened a restaurant.

The boy made a Crunchy Duck so crunchy and ducky a girl began to

QUACK QUACK QUACK

His Creme Caramel was so cremey and caramelly, a customer licked the table.

A man drank soup straight from the bowl so he could clap.

A couple loved their Spaghetti Marinara so much they kissed the spaghetti.

And the most important restaurant critic in the world said the food was so scrump-diddly-icious that everyone in the universe simply had to try it.

Boy was a hit!

Until one night, on the busiest night of the year...

16

...the boy was keeping track of so many different recipes that he started to get confused.

He put
a chicken leg
in an ice
cream sundae.

He put
hot chocolate
in a salad.

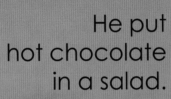

He put
his mother
on a plate of lentils.

Customers sent
their dishes back
to the kitchen.

18

The boy's jaw dropped – it started to quiver. His eyes closed and he started to cry. His fingers curled into fists. His feet stomped on the floor.

The boy threw back his head and screamed louder than anyone had ever screamed before.

Plates started to rattle.
Walls started to shake.
Customers held their ears.
Then they held other customers' ears.
Then they ran out of the restaurant, yelling,
"That kid is screaming so loud I can't eat!"

20

The boy's parents gave him a Time Out.
He screamed.

They gave him a Time In.
He screamed.

They gave him toys.
He screamed.

They took away his toys.
He screamed.

Nothing could make him stop
until his mother said, "That's it.
We won't be screamed at anymore.
If you scream each time something goes
wrong, we'll have to close the restaurant."

He saw the startled customers and worried waiters.
He saw his parents feeling frustrated.

And instead of screaming...he sang.

I'M SOOORRYYYYy

His parents smiled. They gave him a taste
of linguini that was so luscia-licious
the boy lay down on the floor
and fell asleep for a week.

When he awoke, the boy started to cook.
Magical dishes came from the pots and pans and squeezers and freezers.

Word spread that The Screaming Chef was screaming no more, and customers came pouring back in.

A woman loved the Sea-food Paella so much she jumped in the fish tank and swam with the fishes.

A man got one whiff of the sweet and sour dumplings and ran in the kitchen to eat them straight from the pot.

A girl tasted the molten chocolate lava cake, jumped up and recited the alphabet in Swahili. (And she didn't even know Swahili.)

And the next time something went wrong and the boy felt that screamy feeling coming on, he took one look at his parents...

...and he sang. Now instead of running away from The Screaming Chef, people applaud...

The Singing Chef.